HC

D0334478

HARTLEPOOL BOROUGH LIBRARIES WITHDRAWN

HARTLEPOOL BOROUGH LIBRARIES

The Adventures of Benjamin Bear

Claire Freedman
Illustrated by Steve Smallman

1655596 1

Written by Claire Freedman
Illustrated by Steve Smallman

Copyright © 2013 Lion Hudson/Tim Dowley Associates

All rights reserved
No part of this publication may be
reproduced or transmitted in any form or by any means,
electronic or mechanical, including photocopy, recording,
or any information storage and retrieval system, without
permission in writing from the publisher.

Published by Candle Books
an imprint of
Lion Hudson plc
Wilkinson House, Jordan Hill Road,
Oxford OX2 8DR, England
www.lionhudson.com/candle

ISBN 978 1 85985 982 7
e-ISBN 978 1 78128 088 1

First edition 2013

A catalogue record for this book
is available from the British Library

Printed and bound in China, June 2013, LH06

Contents

Benjamin Bear

Says Sorry

The sun shone brightly. Bees buzzed happily.
And little Benjamin Bear felt full of bounce!

"Hooray!" he cried, skipping down the hill. "This is my favourite kind of day for having fun."

Down by the stream, Benjamin's friend Snippy was doing a bit of fishing.

"That looks fun!" Benjamin cried, rushing across. "Can I try?"

Snippy handed over his fishing rod.
"Careful, Benjamin!" he cried. "Mind where you're swinging it!"

Oh no! Benjamin accidentally sent Snippy's hat flying into the stream!

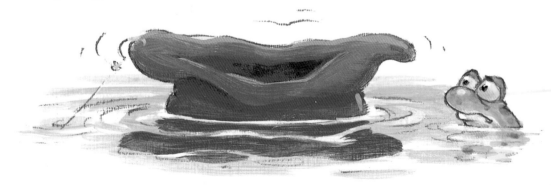

"Whoops!" Benjamin gasped. "How did that happen? I'd better have fun doing something else." And he hurried off.

10

"Huh!" sighed Snippy, wading into the water to fetch his hat. "It would have been nice if Benjamin had said sorry!"

Further downstream, Benjamin found his friend Lofty building sand pies.

"Oooh, that's fun!" Benjamin said. "Can I help?"

"Of course, Benjamin," Lofty replied.

Benjamin started digging excitedly.

Sand flew everywhere!

"Hey, watch out!" cried Lofty.

"You're sending that my way!"

"Whoops!" Benjamin said. "I forgot you were behind me, Lofty. I'll go and have fun somewhere else."

Away he scampered.

"Huh!" sighed Lofty, brushing himself down. "It would have been nice if Benjamin had said sorry!"

Benjamin decided to find a big tree to climb. That was fun too! He clambered up through the branches of a huge oak tree.

"Oh look!" he giggled. "There's Stripe down there. I know – I'll give him a funny surprise!"

Boo!

Benjamin popped his head out through the leaves.

"BOO!" he shouted at the top of his voice.

"Help!" gasped Stripe, leaping up with a start.

"Oh Benjamin – you gave me a scare. I was fast asleep!"

"Whoops, I thought you were awake!" Benjamin said. He jumped down and rushed off.

"Huh!" sighed Stripe. "It would have been nice if Benjamin had said sorry!"

Benjamin whistled cheerfully as he bounced along.
Sniff, sniff! He could smell something delicious –
strawberry bushes!

"Yummy!" he said. "I'll pick some strawberries for tea."

Soon Benjamin had gathered a nice little pile of fruit.
He sat down for a rest when… *Ding-a-ling!* Someone came
whizzing along on their tricycle.

"Mind my strawberries!" Benjamin shouted.

Too late! The cyclist rode right over them!
"Huh!" said Benjamin crossly. "I know that was an
accident. But it would have been nice if he'd said sorry!"

23

Suddenly Benjamin thought.
"Oh dear!" he gulped.
"I never said sorry to Snippy or
Lofty or Stripe – did I? I upset
them by accident too."

But it wasn't too late to put that right. Benjamin quickly picked more strawberries, and raced back to find his friends.

25

"I'm sorry!" he told them.

"That's alright, Benjamin," his friends answered, looking much happier. "We know you didn't mean it."

"Hooray!" cried Benjamin. Suddenly he felt full of bounce again!

Then, happily, the four friends sat down and picnicked on Benjamin's scrummy strawberries.

And together they watched the sun go down on a lovely summer's day.

Benjamin Bear decided that having good friends really *was* the best fun of all!

Everybody does things wrong,
We all can make mistakes.
It's easy though, to put things right,
"I'm sorry" is all it takes.

Benjamin Bear

Says Thank You

The sun was up and shining.
Benjamin Bear was up too,
and feeling his happy bouncy self!

"Hooray!" Benjamin said, as he headed for the park. "There's nothing better than a day spent outdoors, playing with friends."

In the park, Benjamin's friend Lofty
was playing football.
"Hello!" he called. "Fancy a game?"

Lofty passed the ball to Benjamin. THWACK!
Benjamin kicked it SO hard, it flew across the field and
landed in some thick bushes.

"Oh no," Benjamin cried. "I've lost your ball, Lofty!"

Just then their friend Fizzy waved to them from beyond the trees.

"I saw where your ball went, Benjamin," she called. "I'll fetch it!"

Moments later, Fizzy brought it over.

36

"Thank you," Lofty smiled at her.
But Benjamin didn't say thank you.
He was too busy practising his kicks.
Fizzy looked rather hurt.

"Benjamin," Lofty whispered to him. "Haven't you forgotten something?"

"What?" asked Benjamin in surprise.

"To say thank you to Fizzy for finding the ball. You don't want to upset her feelings."

"Oh no!" Benjamin gasped.

"Thank you, Fizzy," he said, giving her a big hug.

"That's okay, Benjamin," Fizzy laughed happily, hugging him back.

After playing football, Benjamin,
Lofty, and Fizzy rushed off to the pond.
Stripe was there with a big bag of bread,
feeding the ducklings.

"That looks fun," cried Benjamin bouncily.

"Here," said Stripe, handing everyone some bread.

"Now you can feed the ducklings too."

"Thank you, Stripe," said both Lofty and Fizzy.

But not Benjamin. He was already throwing breadcrumbs.

"Benjamin," Fizzy nudged him. "I think you've forgotten something again."

"What's that?" Benjamin replied, feeling puzzled.
"To thank Stripe for sharing his bread with you,"
Lofty said. "He's looking rather unhappy."

"Oh dear!" Benjamin gasped. He didn't mean to upset his friend.

"Thank you, Stripe," he said.

"That's alright, Benjamin," Stripe said, looking cheerful again.

When the ducks had been fed, Fizzy and Benjamin
decided to play on the swings.

But Flop-Ear and Hoppy had got there first.

"Would you two like a go?" they called kindly, jumping off.

"Thank you," Fizzy said. "We would."

"I love the swings," Benjamin cried, running over excitedly.

But then he stopped, and thought. He'd forgotten something. Something *very* important!

Suddenly Benjamin remembered what it was!

"Thank you for giving us a turn on the swings," Benjamin said to Flop-Ear and Hoppy.

"You're welcome, Benjamin," his friends smiled.

Benjamin felt very pleased with himself
as he swung to and fro – and full of bounce!

And later, when Lofty treated everyone to ice creams, Benjamin was even happier.

"Thank you," he said. "I love ice cream."

"Yes, thank you, Lofty," the others added.

All except for Hoppy.
Hoppy was too busy licking!

51

"Hoppy," Benjamin whispered in his ear. "Haven't you forgotten something?"

"What's that?" Hoppy said.

"To say thank you to Lofty for buying the ice creams."

"Oops, I forgot!" gasped Hoppy. "I hope I haven't upset his feelings. Thank you, Lofty," he said…

… "and thank you, Benjamin, for reminding me,"
Hoppy added. "It's only a little word…"
"But it means a lot!" Benjamin smiled.

Suddenly he felt so bouncy, he had to do a cartwheel – which made all his friends laugh.

But best of all he felt bouncy on the *inside* – which was his happiest feeling of all!

When someone is nice or kind,
It's good to say "thank you",
It shows that you appreciate,
The things they say and do!

Benjamin Bear

Says Please

One morning Benjamin Bear woke up feeling extra bouncy!
"Hooray, it's been snowing!" he shouted excitedly.
"Everything's covered in white."

Benjamin tugged on his bright red boots and rushed outside to play.

Down by the frosty pine trees, Benjamin
saw his friends, Fizzy and Stripe.

They were building the biggest snowman
Benjamin had ever seen.

"Wow, that looks fun!" Benjamin said.
"I love building snowmen."

Before Stripe and Fizzy had time to say anything, Benjamin began scooping up piles of sparkling snow for their snowman's head.

"We're happy for you to help us," Fizzy told Benjamin,
as the little bear added some twigs for the snowman's arms.
"But it is polite to say please first."

Ooops!

"Fizzy and Stripe are right," Benjamin thought
to himself. *"I must remember to say please next time."*

After building their snowman,
Benjamin and his friends scrunched
through the deep snow and up the hill.

Wheee! Suddenly Flop-Ear whizzed
past them on her brand new sledge.

"That looks great fun, Flop-Ear!" Benjamin
cried bouncily. "I bet I could make your sledge
go even faster!"

Before Flop-Ear could say a word,
Benjamin had jumped aboard the sledge.
He held onto Flop-Ear tightly as they
raced downhill together.

"Of course you can ride on my sledge with me, Benjamin," Flop-Ear said breathlessly as they reached the bottom. "But it is polite to say please first."

"Oh no, I forgot again," Benjamin thought
to himself. "I really must remember to say
please next time."

As Benjamin Bear was bouncing through the thick snowdrifts, he spotted his friend Hoppy.

Hoppy had found a big patch of ice under the trees, and was happily slipping and sliding on it.

"What a great skating rink." Benjamin called out.
"It looks lovely and slippery. I'd like a go!"

Benjamin rushed across and slithered straight onto the ice. Very soon he fell over in a laughing heap.

Hoppy helped him up.

"You're welcome to slide on my ice patch with me,"
Hoppy told Benjamin. "But it is polite to say please first."
"Oh," Benjamin thought to himself. "*I really meant to
say please this time. How ever could I have forgotten again?*"

After a great time building snowmen, sledging downhill, and sliding on the ice, Benjamin and his friends were feeling very hungry.

"Look!" Benjamin cried. "Snippy has set up a food stall down by the frozen stream."

Everyone's eyes lit up.

Snippy was soon handing round hot sugared doughnuts and steaming mugs of hot chocolate to them all.

The little bear couldn't wait!

He scrunched across the snow as fast as his red boots could take him.

"Yummy, I'd love a delicious doughnut," he told Snippy.
Benjamin held out his paw to take one, when suddenly…
    "Oh, I've just remembered something very important,"
he smiled.

"Please can I have a doughnut and a hot chocolate, Snippy?" Benjamin asked.

Snippy smiled. "Of course you can Benjamin – especially after you said please so nicely."

"Hooray!" cheered Benjamin happily, taking a big bite.
Soon everyone was tucking in and enjoying themselves.

"Benjamin," said his friends, as snowflakes began to fall. "Will you come out and play in the snow with us tomorrow? PLEASE – it's been such fun."

"Of course!" Benjamin laughed, thinking he'd like nothing better. "Seeing that you asked me so politely."

And although it was cold and snowy outside, inside Benjamin Bear felt happy and warm. And full of bounce!

When there's something that you'd like,
It's good to be polite.
If you always say "please" first,
You know you've got it right!

Benjamin Bear

Says Goodnight

The golden sun was setting. Benjamin Bear was
playing with his friends Stripe and Flop-Ear –
and feeling full of bounce!

"Benjamin!" called his big sister Bonnie.
"Mama says it's time to come in for your bath!"

"I'm not ready for my bath!" said Benjamin.
"I'm still far too bouncy!"
Flop-Ear and Stripe got ready to go home.

"It *is* late," said Stripe. "It's time to settle down!"

"Yes!" agreed Flop-Ear. "See you tomorrow, Benjamin!"

Benjamin cheered when he saw his bath.
It was overflowing with bubbles and toys!
"Jump in!" Mama Bear smiled.

"Getting clean is fun!" Benjamin cried, splashing about.
"The warm water will help you feel sleepy," said Bonnie.
"Quiet times are fun too, Benjamin!"

Once he was clean, Mama Bear hugged Benjamin dry and dressed him in his comfy nightclothes.

"I still feel too bouncy for bed!" Benjamin giggled.

Papa Bear came in.

"I'll make you a mug of warm milk!" Papa Bear said. "Then you'll feel a lot sleepier."

"Mmmm," said Benjamin after he'd drunk his milk.
"I still feel bouncy – but in a quieter sort of way!"

"That's good!" Mama Bear laughed,
"Because it's time to clean your teeth!"
"I'll help!" said Bonnie.

"Climb into bed," said Mama Bear. "I'll read you
a story. You'll feel even less bouncy then!"

Benjamin Bear snuggled down and Mama Bear read him a lovely story.

"Quiet times are fun too," said Mama Bear, giving him a cuddle.

"Quiet times are nice!" Benjamin nodded happily,
as Mama Bear tucked his teddy into bed with him.

Papa Bear switched on Benjamin's night light.

"Feeling sleepy yet?" he asked.

Benjamin stifled a yawn. "Yes," he nodded.

"But I'm still a bit bouncy!"

"Let's say your prayers," Papa Bear smiled.
"That will help you go to sleep – knowing God is
looking after you all night."

Benjamin said his prayers with Mama and Papa
then snuggled down deeper.

"You must be feeling very sleepy now, Benjamin?"
asked Mama Bear.

Benjamin Bear shook his head.

"I still feel a teeny bit bouncy," he whispered. "Sing me a lullaby, Mama!"

Mama Bear tucked Benjamin up nice and tight, so the covers reached his little nose. Then she sang him a gentle lullaby.

Benjamin struggled to keep his eyes open.
"I do like quiet times, Mama," he said,
"– almost as much as bouncy ones!"

"Quiet times are very special," Mama Bear said with a smile. "A bedtime kiss and cuddle will make you feel even sleepier!"

Mama Bear gave Benjamin a big goodnight kiss.
"I think you're feeling sleepy now," she said.
Benjamin yawned.

"Night-night, dear Benjamin," Mama and Papa whispered and both tip-toed out.
"Sweet dreams!"

Benjamin Bear didn't hear them. He was already fast asleep. Ssssh!

All was quiet for now…

But tomorrow Benjamin Bear would wake up feeling very happy – and full of bounce again!

Seeing friends and playing games
Is always fun to do;
But snug, sleepy bedtimes
Are very special too!

HARTLEPOOL BOROUGH LIBRARIES